My Mother's Pearls

story and art by

Catherine Myler Fruisen

ISBN 0-7683-2177-8

Published in 2000 by Cedco Publishing Company
100 Pelican Way, San Rafael, California 94901
For a free catalog of other Cedco® products, please write to the address
above, or visit our website: www.cedco.com

Book and jacket design by Janice Shay

This is a Design Press book.
Design Press is a division of the Savannah College of Art and Design.

Printed in China

1 3 5 7 9 10 8 6 4 2

For Marianne,
Dede, Anne, Joan, Rita,
and Graiken.

I love getting dressed up with my mom. On those special days, she calls me in early to get ready. The house smells wonderful, because she's already taken a bath with scented bubbles.

I love to watch Mom put on lipstick and perfume.

I do NOT love taking my own bath, but I will, if Mom promises not to pick out her dress without me.

I t's fun helping her choose which dress she'll wear, and I love zipping up her zipper. And I love, love, LOVE helping her clasp her pearls.

They're not just any pearls. They are the FAMILY PEARLS!

When my mom was a little girl like me, her mother Marianne (my grandmother) wore the pearls on special days, too—like my mom's first piano recital.

Mom loved getting dressed up with Grandma Marianne just as much as I love getting dressed up with Mom. And Grandma Marianne told her lots of stories about the pearls. I love it when my mom tells these stories to me!

1 9 6 8

When Grandma Marianne was a little girl, her mother Anna (my great-grandmother) hardly ever took the pearls out of their box. Times were hard then, and ladies did not show off their jewelry.

But on Marianne's sixth birthday, Great-Grandma Anna wore the family pearls while she took Marianne downtown to pick out a special first-day-of-school outfit. They chose a beautiful blue polka-dot dress. As a special treat, Marianne got to wear the dress home.

When Anna was about my age, she did a naughty thing. She played dress-up with her mother's pearls, and broke the string!

Her mother Dede (my great-**great**-grandmother) found all the pearls but one. Somewhere in an old house there's a hidden pearl. I sure hope someone finds it someday.

After that, Great-Great-Grandma Dede wore her pearls all the time— even to bed! Anna was not allowed to touch the pearls until she was grown up. There were lots of ways she could help her mother dress, though.

When Dede was a little girl, she and her family came to America all the way from Scotland to start a new life. Before they left, her mother Rose (my great-**great**-**great**-grandmother) hid the pearls in a secret compartment in her trunk for safekeeping. For three weeks, those pearls were curled in a little box as they sailed across the ocean. They've traveled more than I have!

1878

When Rose was a little girl, her mother Sophie (my great-great-great-great-grandmother, whew!) was a talented seamstress. She made all of her own dresses to show off her favorite pearl necklace. She also made beautiful dresses for Rose… and a necklace of satin covered buttons, so Rose could pretend to wear pearls, too.

When Sophie was a little girl, ladies dressed very delicately. Sophie's mother Violet, my great-great-great-great-great-grandmother, always wore pearls…even on lazy afternoons in the garden.

And Violet's mother Susanna (my great-great-great-great-great-great-Grandmother) wore the pearls every evening. She would play the piano and sing for little Violet.

And guess what? Great-Great-Great-Great-Great-Great-Grandma Susanna's pearls were a wedding gift from her husband. The inscription on the box read, *Pearls for my Pearl.*

So Susanna gave them to Violet on her wedding day, who gave them to Sophie, who gave them to Rose, who gave them to Dede, who gave them to Anna, who gave them to Marianne, my Grandma. And Grandma Marianne gave those very pearls to my mother on her wedding day. She was a beautiful bride!

I have my own set of pearls. Mom lets me wear them when it's my turn to get dressed up. They're not real, but I love them because they make me think about all of my grandmothers. I wonder if they knew how many mothers and daughters would wear the pearls?

Who do **you** think will wear them next?